SHUTAO LIAO

STORIES OF ROARS

Copyright © 2023 by Shutao Liao

All rights reserved. No part of this publication may be reproduced, stored or transmitted in any form or by any means, electronic, mechanical, photocopying, recording, scanning, or otherwise without written permission from the publisher. It is illegal to copy this book, post it to a website, or distribute it by any other means without permission.

Second edition

*This book was professionally typeset on Reedsy.
Find out more at reedsy.com*

Contents

STORIES OF ROARS	1
Preface	5
1. A Sarcastic Being	9
2. The Jungle World	13
3. The Rise of Roars	17
4. More About The Roarers	20
5. Dancing With A Skeleton Lover	22
6. The Elongated Shadow	28
7. A True Story of A Cat	31
8. The Card House	36
9. The Decay of Beauty	42
10. The Mask Man	47
11. The Pigeons	51
12. The Witch	55
13. The Station	61
14. A Tortured Soul	65
15. The Nights Were Moving	69
16. The Prophecy	77
17. Conversation With A Hermit	80
18. The Kids	86
19. The Wanderer	89
20. The Day	96
21. The Bell	104
Epilogue	106

About the Author 108

STORIES OF ROARS

Shutao Liao

STORIES OF ROARS

We may get through, may not get through, it depends.

STORIES OF ROARS

If society abandoned its people, people could ignore society as well.

This book is a tribute to Schopenhauer
for his deep insight into the ugly nature of human beings
and the plight of human destiny.

STORIES OF ROARS

If society abandoned its people, people could ignore society as well.

Preface

If you want to comprehend the critical contemporary life, you need to read this book.

I regard myself as a surgeon when writing this book, my intention is to show the wounds and damage of the present society. In those sick years, the split of human nature and pain in society were so deep, and also so widespread. The stories in this book are only a slice of present painstaking life revealed by the author. To overlook or deny them means living in lies. Having pain is good for finding out the bottom line a human being can suffer. We may get through, may not get through, it depends.

This is a psychic description about the reality and beyond the reality. Timid readers, please prepare yourselves for the coming encounters!

There was a spiritual walker whose routine daily schedule was going to bed at six in the morning, which meant whose life activities were mainly based on nightlife. Naturally who saw unusual things happened more than other people, recently becoming more and more tragic, more and more intense. The most impressive happening was the roars, which were everywhere in the city, sometimes like lion's, sometimes as bear's, occasionally similar to hyena's. The roars were like a disease spreading so rapidly around here, the place I was talking about was New York City, the city of roars, the birth of rebellious souls.

If you didn't know the roars, you didn't know real New York even you had lived here for decades, because you were staying on the surface of the city life, did not touch the psychic level which had made this city to a drama generator, a jungle field displaying everything from minor mischief to tragic meaningless deaths. The dividing line between the nature of humans and the nature of animals had disappeared. The roars seemingly were overwhelming all over the city. Those stories happening in this book were nothing about the good or the bad, just overflowing as nature went, also which were nothing about beasts, animals, or ghosts and vampires. They were about something that actually happened, from odd appearances to the deep inside out, they were not fantasies, but much more fantasies than a fantasy could carry, and they were real!

In the whole human history, one truth never changed: The weak were slaughtered or slaved by the strong, and the strong defined what was the meaning of justice with whatever means, who always covered their evil intentions with the colorful images of an angel. The aftermath was the birth of roarers, those who

Preface

disregarded the established social rules, acting according to their own will.

Certainly the roarers were produced by the cruelty and torment of contemporary human life. Maybe you are a roarer which you don't know. After you finish reading this book, you will find out the conclusion. Even if you are not a roarer, you still need to look through this book, because nowadays it is impossible to walk around the city without encountering the danger of a roarer. It will be a very disadvantageous situation if you encounter roarers who you know nothing about.

The protagonists introduced in this book were in New York, but could be anywhere in the world.

STORIES OF ROARS

The aftermath was the birth of roarers, those who disregarded the established social rules, acting according to their own will.

1. A Sarcastic Being

I didn't know from which time I was already being a dreaming walker, others called me a weirdo, since then, noticed a lot of things which I hadn't known before. One day when I saw a huge, heavy cloud setting itself down on Brooklyn Bridge, I said to myself: "This is a big omen."

It was so clear that I did not have any association with those who were so wrong as well as so rude, defining me as a weirdo, only because of the fact that I could see the others could not perceive so I was a weirdo? Only because of the fact that those so-called "normal" people who were blind to the fact and the happenings of this world I became a weirdo? Only because of the fact that I was able to feel and touch the truth beneath the surface of so defined reality l became a weirdo, if so, yes! I am a weirdo.

Oh please don't talk to me about the museums and the galleries in the city, please don't talk to me about what they were doing and what had on their shows, for only God knew what in their minds of the organizers and what were going on inside those huge buildings which themselves were much better than the objects showing to the public. When events organizers were standing in front of audiences talking about the shows curated, I could see everything inside and outside of their appearing: I saw their hyper body blood flowing; I saw their naked bodies shaking with groans; I saw sexual hormone growing inside their glands; I saw the paradise that was forbidden and the door of the hell was opened since they were only cells carrying existing rules from the famous institutions such as Harvard or Princeton where the vivid humane culture already buried, replacing by cold rules that were exactly against the real interest of living mankind. I was not someone against culture, instead, was a culturally rooted human being who was unfortunately in real love with culture that made me sad instead of happy for the ongoing. Dear readers, only thinking about those real situations could generate immense pain in my heart, unbearable because I could not shut off my emotional door to block those facts, also because I was sincere and real.

For those who were happy about being manipulated by the system didn't even know they were being manipulated, there was not a single bridge between me and them to hold their hands, "sympathy" was my word preserved for those miserable existing souls. I was deeply saddened for them because I was not an indifferent person that was why I got deep sorrow in my heart. After all, we all were small creatures climbing on the surface of earth to survive. Even though I felt isolated from the others and felt good in such a condition. There were still some who were rejecting the current events of museums and galleries,

1. A Sarcastic Being

struggling for their individualities, who were the people I was addressing, and they could follow my words to the next story of this book.

Before going to the next story, I wanted to remind you: Please do not look for happiness in this devastated world, it was dangerous! You would feel truly tormented by the search. the seed of happiness planted inside of your physical body at the moment when you were born, yourself, not any other ones, were responsible to cultivate it, preserve it in your own soul, and make it flourish.

The real protagonists in this book were not me, but the roarers, it was better I retreated behind the curtains.

STORIES OF ROARS

I didn't know from which time I was already being a dreaming walker, others called me a weirdo, since then, noticed a lot of things which I hadn't known before.

2. The Jungle World

More than three hundred years ago, if any adventurers were sailing from the Arctic Ocean down to the south, passing through Greenland, crossing Labrador Sea, then Nova Scotia; if they were heading down from Northwestern Passages, a little bit west, to cross the immense Hudson Bay, both were extremely difficult voyages, more tragic than you could imagine, actually which were impossible voyages even today! Beside the extremely cold weather, there were countless huge icebergs, the boundless wildness covered with hard, thick layers of snow, wild jungles with various brutal beasts, swamps carrying undiscovered diseases, made no one dare to challenge to travel between those regions on earth. Luckily there was another passage from the east to the west across North Atlantic Ocean, as the English did, to reach this part of the earth, the thousands of miles of vast islands covered with thick forests, hanging at the east corner of the huge North America Continent, the striking psychological evaluation of beings was about to happen, and it would be told in this book, and that was playing a key role in this world where was the home of all mankind.

The people who had been living here before the English came were the indigenous Indian tribes such as Wecquaesgeek, Cayuga, Mohawk, Oneida, Onondaga, Seneca, Tuscarora etc.. Those people believed that the soul would never die, the death itself was only a transition to another journey. Because of this, they were very careful about how to handle the dead, who could be buried above ground on a scaffold or a tree, or by cremation and mummification, sometimes the bones were saved, and a rich mass burial ritual was conducted, caves and fissures in rocks were used to inter the dead. Some buried the owner's horses and dogs with the body, and in some cases, the corpse was immediately buried, and the house of the dead burnt so that the spirit might not return. People were dancing with special chanting to demonstrate grief, memories as well as respect to the dead. That was an arcane journey into the spiritual world of the Native Americans of North America.

The Indians played a clarinet or a flute to communicate with nature, overflowing their spirit as well as thoughts in the purified sound, they talked with nature because they believed that all things had spirit: the sun, the moon, sky, clouds, wind, rivers; trees, grass, plants; bears, wolves, birds, eagles, nightingales and owls and so on.

When at the first time they saw the huge British ships anchored on the shores of this eastern part continent, they knew something unusual would happen, but they never anticipated the worst was coming. After countless bloody kills, they

2. The Jungle World

fled to the remote barren areas of the west to escape their deadly tragedies. Just at that time, the first generation of self unconscious roarers was coming into human life, a gesture to be helplessly free, independent, and indifference about the fact that the frangibility as a being, intentionally avoiding or going away from all social systems, which was a sense of self protection, a psycho infection, silently growing inside a being, evolving itself throughout the time, to the era we were living after hundreds of years, extremely contagious, spreading to every human society. At that time there were a lot of kills, hundreds of thousands of human corpses and dead horses with their big round bellies floating on the rivers, until the water became as red as dusk, bloody views! The bloody floats were lasting hundreds of years, to the so-called civilized brutal world of the present day. The roars generated from the bloody rivers, reaching far away in time, waiting for us to encounter. Since then, even no one saw them, which stayed with us, multiplied quickly until psychologically contaminated a lot of human lives in societies. Thus we called those rejective souls as roarers.

STORIES OF ROARS

At that time there were a lot of kills, hundreds of thousands of human corpses and dead horses with their big round bellies floating on the rivers, until the water became as red as dusk, bloody views!

3. The Rise of Roars

In another dimension, our creator was coldly watching us, no slightest kindness would be overlooked, no slightest evil intention would let it go without punishment at The Final Judgment, everything put together of what we did would build up our fate. He saw our stupidity in the tricky cleverness, with a big sigh.

When the darkness fell, Brooklyn Bridge put its own shadow heavily upon the Hudson River. Fog appeared slowly on its surface, moving like snakes, spreading itself along the shores, meanwhile the spirit of roars came out from the water on earth. The surroundings were in absolute silence. People already went to sleep in the city, no one knew what was going on here, only the stars hanging over the deep sky kept watching downward.

The spirit of roars was shapeless, tasteless and invisible, its movement was also soundless, only occasionally the clear sound of the flowing water broke out of the stillness. To detect its existence, we as human beings needed a third eye which we didn't have.

Those micro particles carried invisible chemicals contaminating creatures including people. They were spreading in the air we breathe, looking for rejective souls. After being contaminated, They would change the psychological conditions of thinking, and also human feelings, then those with the chemical contamination would become roarers. Because of the pressure of modern social life, and the evolution of nature, which changed people from inside out.

Tonight, in the deadly calmness, all of a sudden, a heartbreaking scream burst out in one dark window, thrusting itself deeply into the night sky, echoed in the open space, responded here and there, teared off the surface of the silence. Another person was captured, another roarer was born.

One thing was clear that whenever and wherever was a torture happened, would give a chance for a roarer to come into life. Who exactly knew?

The journey of torture already began.

3. The Rise of Roars

One thing was clear that whenever and wherever was a torture happened, would give a chance for a roarer to come into life. Who exactly knew?

4. More About The Roarers

Generally speaking, a roarer would make roars, but not every roarer making roars, some never made even one roar in their entire lives but they were still roarers, and also, not everyone who experienced a torture could become a roarer, which made the contaminating psycho infection become a very delicate word. The only thing I could tell you was that a roarer had to have a strong character. If you felt abandoned, neglected, oppressed, unsatisfied, unjustified by the existing world, felt indifference and the intentional desire of rejection to the existing standard values as well as social rules, going to a pretend direction with the self determined will, you had the potential to be one of them.

I might have talked too much, let the protagonists embark on the stage!

4. More About The Roarers

The only thing I could tell you was that a roarer had to have a strong character.

5. Dancing With A Skeleton Lover

That day was a gray day, the ground was wet, an aftermath of the rain last night. Occasionally wild cats or dogs were running across the bare streets, playing with the leaves in the wind, sneaking into shrubs and the fences of houses, watching people passing by with extra caution, they did not have any trust to human's behavior. A feeling of anxiety was overflowing all the time in the air.

Huge clouds like swollen monsters engulfed the tops of the buildings in the city; flying birds suddenly bumped themselves to the branches of trees, or killed themselves by dashing to the ground; yellow leaves were falling in the echoes of the roars here and there. Last night, people found many dead bodies of different creatures, both humans and animals under the huge structures of Queensboro Plaza which were made of steel and cement. Years before people had found a large crack in the middle of the bridge, which was like being torn by the powerful beast's claws, but no one knew what it was! The repair went

5. Dancing With A Skeleton Lover

through three years with dozens of construction workers to fix the damage. Since then the scary feeling captured people's hearts around the city, always worried something bad was going to happen, indeed something very bad was about to fall on the faces of people here. Screams were shaking the city with horror which people genuinely loved, could you imagine people loved to be scared? Since they didn't want to, and also didn't believe in so-called normal life anymore, and they were very sick, they simply could not afford happy stories which were against their real life situations.

There was a feeling of ecstasy close to the nearby areas of death, creatures carrying psychological drama with them.

Mr. Juan O Savin liked the dramatic change of the weather. He had had a good life only when his wife Berta was alive. The day when she passed away, he cried his heart out, the good life was over, and the purpose of life had gone. At the funeral, he thrust himself over Berta's dead body, sobbing with intense quiver, squeezing her body which he had used to sleep with, wishing to recover her consciousness. Several men had to use full strength to separate them, he still grasped the coffin in desperation, people saw blood running out from his fingernails, left red prints on the wood surface. After the last shovel of earth over the coffin, he became a soulless being, a walking dead, for his soul was also buried with Berta.

He would sit down in the empty rooms for hours without a single move, and stopped cooking, searching food in the trash cans nearby on the streets. Although he stopped crying, but felt his heart was bleeding, could not perceive anything in front of his eyes, which automatically changed to the figure of Berta, who sometimes was smiling at him, greeting him; sometimes was mad with him for he had made himself so dirty without washing. more and more wrinkles climbed over his face, and hairs wildly grew until they covered most of his face, which looked much older than his age. Occasionally a thunder-like roar would generate from his throat, echoing in the dark, empty streets, shaking down the leaves in the air. People were scared of him, avoiding him as far as possible. Eventually he stayed the days and nights absolutely alone.

He would go out to visit Berta's tomb, even on stormy nights, shouting her name in the wilderness, the voice was heartbreaking, with hope one day she would come back to him. His eyes were sparkling with ecstasy after the visit. After ten years, at one midnight, he made a crucial decision, brought a shovel with him, trampled to the tomb, dug out of the covering earth. There she was, silently lying flat in the coffin, the flesh had gone, the remains was only a skeleton. He brought that home with hyper excitement. At home, he cleaned those bones with extreme care, regarding them as Berta's naked body, afterwards putting the skeleton on his bed with great joy. After reflecting over death three times each day in one month, he reached his conclusion: "She did not die, but changed her appearance." He said to himself: "There was no such thing as death, people lied to talk in this way."

From then on, he was living with his wife Berta again, holding her bones to sleep with deep love every night, his life became colorful. When they were sitting together on the table for dinner, he would talk to her: "My dear Berta, I know you hate

5. Dancing With A Skeleton Lover

to eat, but don't worry, I will eat for you, you will never need to worry about eating matters."

He felt sunshine fall upon his face again, singing romantic songs with a tender voice for hours. Sometimes an unconscious smile would appear on his face, when the neighbors saw his smiling face, they looked at him as a real monster.

About three months later, one day suddenly he had an inspiration, dressed her up in a colorful skirt with luscious decorations, he even put a beautiful straw hat over the skull with lovely flowers. Then he held the skeleton to dance in the backyard with the melodies of love, like the old days, both of them had loved dancing very much. It's obviously awkward at the beginning, luckily he was a genius in dancing, after one month of practice, Berta became alive. He tenderly held her waist, They danced together like real lovers, vividly with passion, their movements showing a special elegance, better than two persons in the dance. His joy was beyond words to describe. He was dancing day in and day out. After a while, it turned out to be an eye-catching magic, no one saw him dancing without stopping to enjoy, the skeleton was moving more elegantly as well as lividly than a real lady. To Mr. Juan O Savin, it was a real woman, the only one he truly loved in his life.

He turned himself into a proud man, no one in the world had such a beauty as he composed. He would put his head high in the air like a king in front of people, dressed himself with luscious full dresses, a formal hat, a purple bow tie, and perfect shining shoes.

STORIES OF ROARS

When he was traveling around the city, always carrying his lover in a suitcase. It's time to show off. After choosing a good location like a plaza or a subway station to dance, he would play romantic music while dancing, instantly people would form a large crowd around him, amused and cheerful, above all, amazed. After all nothing in the world could be so magic as this dashing dancing. His name was soaring with people's mouths, he became a hero of our times.

He changed into another man, a man filled with permanent love, a man who conquered death, a man who turned tragedy into beauty, a man whose touch turned ashes into a living flower, a man whose romance was beyond words to describe, a man whose joy and satisfaction was everlasting.

He traveled everywhere. At first, around the city, then going further and further, until his footprints were all over this nation. When came back home, he always held his lover during the night. Sometimes tears shed from the corners of his aged eyes, not because of pain, but from an appreciation of deep love.

5. Dancing With A Skeleton Lover

After a while, it turned out to be an eye-catching magic, no one saw him dancing without stopping to enjoy, the skeleton was moving more elegantly as well as lividly than a real lady.

6. The Elongated Shadow

Last night, I did not hear any roars, it was unusual for such a night. I am sitting by the window, serving myself with a cup of coffee. It is a quiet morning, only several crows are hovering in the sky. I am enjoying the view outside of my window, even though all I can see are empty sky and the silhouette of the top parts of buildings. Actually I am waiting for the New York Times and New York Post which I ordered for daily morning reading to capture the tides of life. I always check on the Death Notice, and search for local news for what happened yesterday. At this moment I am unconsciously falling into daydreams, my mind is floating with the tragic events for the past decades in the city. With a cigar in my hand, my thoughts are following Its dancing smoke to the outside of the window. The ringing bell of the front door puts me back to reality. The delivery man is at the front door of my house.

We met so frequently, regarding each other as old friends. He is an old fashioned man, has a big mustache, wearing a pair

6. *The Elongated Shadow*

of brown glasses attached with a safety chain around the back of his reddish ears. Today when I see him, his face is as pale as the dead, and eyes are in dismay: " Sir, Re, Really tragic! Real tragedy happened!" Only those few words already have exhausted his effort to say what he knows about. I watch him with deep sympathy.

It is said in the newspapers that people found many dead bodies last night at different locations: beside Hudson River; under the dark shadows of Brooklyn Bridge as well as Queens Bridge; Bronx and Coney Island. There is an atmosphere of horror in the minds of local people: What the hell is going on here day by day?

Since the beginning of this year, more and more dead creatures, not only people, were found in the city all over the five boroughs, the numbers were increasing rapidly. Ambulances were whirling day and night, corpses were piled up in the long frozen containers on the streets outside of every hospital.

The top doctors as well as medical experts have studied the cases with all the efforts but failed to find what had caused so many deaths. There was one symptom in common, most of the dead creatures had a broken throat but that wasn't enough to kill them. What they did not know was those dead creatures were roarers, their deaths were the results of psychological craziness.

Unfortunately we are living in an era of psychological corruption, the helplessness and alienation of mankind.

Unfortunately we are living in an era of psychological corruption, the helplessness and alienation of mankind.

7. A True Story of A Cat

We, cats, have the same structure of tigers, very unfortunately because of the size differences, we have totally different life stories.

I was born at a pet center somewhere in the Bronx, people built cages to keep us inside, that meant from the beginning of my life, I already lost my freedom as a living being, destined to be a property of someone. People thought the fact that they kept us as pets provided us a good life, the real issue was that they never considered cats needed to be free in nature. I grew up there until I was adopted by a lady.

I felt really assaulted when people said to someone: "you are as bad as an animal!" As if we were the worst living beings, I felt like vomiting by hearing such nonsense. Did you see any animals lying to each other as human beings? Did you see any animals killing each other as human beings? Did you see any animals as cruel as human beings? Did you see any animals hurting each other only for the reason of self enjoyment as human beings? They destroyed other species until nearly extinguished, then built so-called "Reservations" to "protect" them; they honored their soldiers for killing; they did most damage to nature until they felt in danger of themselves then proclaimed to save the world. We, animals only did the kills for food to survive, insulted other animals only for protection of our own lives and cubs. Once I was passing by a slaughterhouse, I was shocked by the desperate screams of the cows and pigs. They never considered how animals felt when they were killing them. They also invented so many tools to torture each other. The wars between humans were basically the largest scale of lawful mutual slaughter. They could not live on without mutual hatred as well as mutual torment. Could you imagine the cruelty? Could you imagine how they dealt with each other? Could you imagine how ridiculous? The slavery system had gone, but most people were still being slaved to struggle for their basic needs by a few. Although the wealth of the world was enough for all people out of poverty, there were still a lot of hungry people. They invented countless weapons only for easier slaughter, what does that mean? They were getting closer to destroying each other completely. They made every creature on earth in danger, not to mention they created viruses spreading all over the world. We, animals never hated each other unless there was an obvious reason, human beings had a long way to go to reach our animal level of behavior. The development of their science might be fast, but thinking about the evolution of their morality which was extremely slow, no difference than thousands of years before. In public they acted beautifully as angels, they had to lie to hide their true nature and to cover their dirty minds.

7. A True Story of A Cat

As in the case of my mistress, the lady who kept me. I watched her behavior closely with my open eyes. When she was dressed up, I had to admit that she was beautiful! I had no doubt a lot of men would be allured by her innocent appearance. One day a man went into her bedroom, they didn't know I was hidden under the bed, or didn't care, I heard their moans clearly while they were copulating. After the dramatic bed action, she swore that she would love him forever. I was so touched by her words which showed the emotional beauty of human love in front of my own eyes! To my surprise, another man came several days later, and she said exactly the same words to him. If I didn't know what had happened before, I would be touched. At that time, I only felt disgusted! Those shameless moments repeated time and time again, since then I understood human nature much better, they never could stop lying in their lives for selfish desires.

My mistress aroused my curiosity as a specimen to study the nature of human behavior, so I decided to follow her to find out more about her life. Recently my mistress had a big problem, she was quarreling with one of her lovers more and more often even though they had had very sweet moments before. Who was Mr. Elliott, a carefully shaved man, with a well designed mustache, and tattoos all over the body, whose forearms had images of skulls, which were an unfortunate omen. One day when my mistress was with her new lover Juan, after a passionate moment, she talked about Mr. Elliott to him. They decided to do something to fix the problem.

It was a stormy night, with heavy downpours as well as lightning, twigs bumped window panes in the howling of wind.

STORIES OF ROARS

I heard there were urgent knocks on the front door. It was Mr. Elliott, when my mistress opened the door, he rushed in along with the gush of the rain in the dark. What he did not know was that Juan was hidden behind the door, who jumped over and stabbed him on the belly with a sharp knife, blood was gushing from the body, splashed all over the floor. Juan looked down coldly over Mr. Elliott's dead body, kicked it several times with strong hatred as well as contempt. I was totally shocked by what I saw. They dragged the dead body to the backyard, buried with a shovel. I saw green light sparkling in my mistress's eyes, who was in a high mood of satisfaction.

Juan became a regular visitor of my mistress, they made love together, joked together and laughed together. The storm in life had gone, replaced with peace and joy, but not for long, Juan met the same fate as Mr. Elliott when my mistress found another lover. The story repeatedly continued, after several years the backyard was buried with a dozen dead men. My mistress planted colorful flowers there, which seemed like a cozy place to rest, especially in the spring. The flowers were waving in the gentle breezes, bees were flying, stopped here and there, a lovely scene to feel at home.

At the same time, my mistress never discontinued her hunt for men.

7. A True Story of A Cat

My mistress aroused my curiosity as a specimen to study the nature of human behavior, so I decided to follow her to find out more about her life.

8. The Card House

I never stopped keeping an eye on the column of the Death Notice and the Missing People in the New York Post to find out the ongoing tragedies in the city, from that I could analyze the human psychological corruption condition of social life. That afternoon, I was looking down to the city, Hudson River as still as dead. I was thinking if we really had the original sin as human beings, it's because we depended on eating other lives to survive, the more sinful was that we killed lives for emotional reasons or desires.

It was not a surprise all things were going on at The Card House: the roars here and there, curses from angry men as well as women, even you could hear the clear moans from people who were copulating upstairs and downstairs. Those days people were living a transparent life, nothing could be hidden, we were being watched all the time, including those who were living in the neighborhood at The Card House with the fever of emotional tides. Only one place was always kept in silence,

8. The Card House

which was the rooms Ryan was living in.

He was a man six feet tall, strong and clearly shaved, there was a scar beside his left ear, a result from a fierce fight. He had dated a girl who was working at the gas station near where he was living at the age of thirteen. When the darkness fell, he would sneak to the back of the gas station, put the fingers to the mouth, emitting a short, bright whistle, before long the girl would appear silently, looking at him while giggling. She was a good looking chubby girl, having freckles on the nose bridge and both of the cheeks. They went down to the slope and made love there as usual, both of them were very excited with each other, but it did not last long. A few years later, after she left with her uncle to another city, they did not see each other anymore.

He lost his purpose of life, had dreamt with the girl to have a family, and bore some children, but the result became emptiness. He felt tormented, and also betrayed, with the feeling his soul was split into pieces, trampled by the world. For the next few years he was wandering around the five boroughs, intentionally making troubles to people, cursing passersby; throwing balls at the heads of people to play a hit and run game. One time he was caught when he threw a huge rock at the rear pane of a green van, because he had not noticed that the owner of the car was sitting inside, who brought him to court, his father had to appear on the court for the fact that he was only a teenager, the judge, an amiable woman, gave his father five hundred dollars fine, and warned him: "you must pay this gentleman all the money within half a year, otherwise you will have big trouble." The father was furiously angry, who dragged him on the street corner outside the courthouse, served him a good beating. At home even his two younger sisters despised him, keeping distance from him as far as possible. His mother looked at him with painful watery eyes, which filled with love, torment and helpless emotions. He could not bear to see her anymore, just wanted to hide himself in the world. He grew up with an indifferent attitude to the society rules.

A strong storm called Nova was formed at Mexico Gulf, reaching New York City from the south after Maryland swept the five boroughs with heavy torrential rain last night. Huge waves immersed houses by the Long Island shores, dead bodies floating in the water, allured some bears as well as wolves living in the jungle to eat the flesh of the dead. In the city during the night, the sharp sounds of the bumping windows, cracking window panes, broken branches of trees made continued dismay, waking up people in the nightmares. When daybreak, people were astonished by the views of dead cats, dogs and corpses of people hanging over the bare tree branches. The sky darkened by a huge cloud of crows flying by, some pieces of flesh falling from their beaks, people were screaming in shock at the view.

"This world is fucked up bro!" Ryan talked to himself. He decided to add a little bit of a tragic ingredient to the city today, which made him feel an intimate ecstasy.

After the storm, it was an unusually calm day, nature even impressed people with a lyric feeling. Behind the rolling clouds, bright sunshine spread cheerful bright colors all over the sky. Ryan went down to the street, there was a Deli Cafe grocery

8. The Card House

shop nearby, he bought a coffee and a piece of bread as breakfast, then strolling along Queens Blvd, turned to Broadway. There were three cops standing at the entrance of Elmhurst Station, he shouted at them with dirty curses, they did not bother to move, putting hands in their pockets. Nowadays cops were doing nothing to most crime actions due to the sensitive racial issues which was a real pity.

He went down to the station, there was an old man singing soft melodies on the platform, which reminded him of the old days with the girl he loved, tears went down from his face, he threw one dollar to the suitcase by the singer. It was crowded in the car, which was a surprise to him on such a dreary day. Maybe because of the rush hours, or people were indifferent to the tragedies. Some passengers had to stand. There were three Mexicans wearing traditional wide straw hats, one of them immediately sang, the other two playing guitar. After that several black kids were dancing, jumped on the poles to demonstrate some difficult movements. Few people donated money for the shows, people were poor themselves, did not have too much money to help. Ryan got off at 14 street station, strolling eastward to the Greenwich area, he put the hoodie over his head. Some people were passing by him hastily, he waited until he only saw a man in front of him. At that moment he increased the speed, when he was side by side with the man, suddenly he took out a knife thrust into the man's belly, he fell down to the ground, his limbs instinctively struggling because of the pain. Ryan gave him some kicks over the belly as well as the head, ran away quickly, and disappeared from the spot.

In the evening Ryan played the pool at Jackson Heights of

Queens with some Spanish strangers, almost forgetting what he had done to the man in the afternoon.

Next day on the New York Post, there was an article which stated:

"On Greenwich Ave, people found a man who was stabbed to death and reported to police. No reason was discovered for the tragic incident, which was the third case in this month. It was believed there was a random serial killer at large. Until the time of the report, no suspect was found, and no one was charged. The tragedy is being investigated by the police…."

There was no safety anymore in the city, it sounded like we were living in the wild jungle world.

8. The Card House

It was not a surprise all things were going on at The Card House.

9. The Decay of Beauty

As I was watching the bloody sunset through my room, which reflected strong shadows on the wall in front of my window, the bare tree branches against the sky created a struggling impression on my mind. No doubt every existing life was a process of struggle. I was thinking the decay of humans had to be linked to their selfish nature.

I first saw Olivia at a bar near the east side of the city on a deep night where I was a regular visitor. She was sitting by the counter near the bartender, shamelessly exposing her large breasts, putting her arms around the shoulders and the heads of two men around her, they were laughing as well as joking all the time. If a man touched her naked body, she would burst out a sharp scream as if she was bitten by a snake.

I silently stayed away from them, but kept an eye on her. She was a blonde with blue eyes, light complexion, a full shaped female body, nearly forty. I knew she was infamous in the

9. The Decay of Beauty

city. Noticing me gazing at her, she pushed the men away and approached me: "Do you like my body?" There was a mock tune in her voice while talking, she squeezed her tits together in front of my very eyes, didn't wait for my answer and replied by herself: "Of course you do!" I hadn't prepared for such a situation at all, she saw me blushed, immediately burst into laughter: "Who are you?" She asked. I said I was a painter, "Well, well painter, I want to give you a commission to do." She continued: "Are you afraid to draw naked people?" I answered: "Do you think an artist has a problem drawing nudes?" She laughed loudly when hearing my words, her bright body was shaking coincidentally in the laughter, shining in the lights. I felt a little bit embarrassed when she stretched her arm around my neck, I was not used to being so close in public to a naked woman.

I had some curiosity, having heard a lot of rumors at the bar about her. "Who really is she?" I asked myself. The other day, I drove to where she was living to draw her, somewhere close to Amitiville on Long Island via Southern State Pkwy, it was a pleasant journey. After an early morning rain, the air seemed very fresh with a sweet scent. I was happy to avoid the noisy daily life in the city, even in a short time, as a nature lover, alway felt at home to see the trees, flowers, even shrubs by the roadsides while driving, not to mention occasionally some wild geese, birds as well as seagulls in view. Not for long, I already reached her place. After ringing the doorbell, she appeared in a transparent silk robe, very feminine and alluring as usual, that time I wasn't surprised because that was her usual personal style, or a typical life attitude. While walking me to a big parlor decorated with lifelike animal specimens and naked statues, two parrots standing on a tropical plant greeted me: "Welcome! Welcome!…" she asked me: "Are you ready to draw me?" I assured her with a "Yes", she returned me a gaily smile. To my surprise, a man coming inside, Olivia introduced him as Mr. Ricardo. Then she said: "I want you to draw us making love." Although I had prepared, I still felt a little bit shocked by her suggestion. I had to admit they performed a passionate copulation in front of me. When Ricardo went inside her body, she showed an expression from anguish to ecstasy on her face, as if her body was broken. I did not know which was more: joy or torment, there was no difference between paradise and hell.

I still went to the bar occasionally, but for a period of time, did not see Olivia. It was said that sometimes she was standing naked at Times Square surrounded by the flow of hundreds of people, greeting them to take photos with her, but barely with any success, it might be that they were scared of her bold attitude. Several months later, a really dark rainy night, cold wind was howling at every corner of the streets. I was quivering when entering the bar, feeling gratitude for having a glass of gin to ease the tension of my soul in the tedious daily life. Few people were in the bar. It was understandable that on such a miserable night, most local fellows preferred to stay at home than come here. A solitary song was floating in the air, the mono female voice could arouse the feeling of sorrow and suffering, no one had an easy life, especially in those dreary days with a lot of tragedies going on in the metropolitan area. Suddenly a woman in a mink coat pushed in, pouring rain and the gust of wind immediately followed her in, shaking the hanging lights in the air. It was Olivia, who neglected me, directly rushed to the counter, sat herself down heavily, gushed for breath. The

9. The Decay of Beauty

waiter served her a glass of wine momentarily. There were bruises on her face, after a few drinks, she buried her face in her hands, sobbing painfully without considering the others: "Fuck the weather! Fuck the city! Fuck the world!" she shouted, with crazy laughter. I quickly finished my gin, it's better to leave here, I already lost the mood of easy calmness, pulled up my coat collar tightly around my neck,, forced myself into the windy darkness in the rain.

What happened afterwards was really tragic. It was said that that very night when Olivia was driving home to Long Island in the rain, she found herself being followed on the highway in the dark, she tried to call for help. A few days later, several kids were playing at the Bay Shore Beach, they came across a human remains, it was her, with dark bruises as well as cuts on the body, it was clear she had been brutally tortured before her death. Beside her corpse, there was a slip of paper writing two words: Human trash!

STORIES OF ROARS

"Do you like my body?" There was a mock tune in her voice while talking, she squeezed her tits together in front of my very eyes, didn't wait for my answer and replied by herself: "Of course you do!"

10. The Mask Man

Nowadays it is impossible for anyone walking around New York City without seeing men carrying shocking music players on streets, they are roarers. Let my introduce the original story, the very first one to you.

Time is like an empty container, because of its emptiness, we can fill it in with all different kinds of legends. If we do something in a short frame of time, it relatively seems easy to perform, but if we do the same thing for a long time, it is obviously quite difficult, and very unusual.

I first saw the musk man more than thirty years ago. At that time, I knew nothing about roars, my heart filled with sunshine, hope, passion, dreams and anticipation to the world. I remembered it was a sunny day. I just got out of the subway, and came across an unusual scene on the street corner: a man around his twenty five wearing a worn out colorless rag, facing a shining glass window to exercise his muscles. His eyes without pupils, only showing two small black dots in the middle, when they looked at you, would arouse a supernatural, inhuman feeling, a feeling of savageness. His dark skinned body was as shining as bronze. There was a music player with a loudspeaker beside him. He stood there working on his muscles in the loud sound for hours, then carrying the player walking away in the gazes of amazed people on the spot. Yes! He was the first roarer I knew in New York. At that time, you could not see as many roarers as recent days carrying loud music players. He was the first one, the pioneer of the music walking lifestyle against established settings of social life. Recently it has already evolved into quite a phenomenon.

In the last decades, all the year round, no matter shining or rainy, hot or cold, day after day, he would appear in Manhattan to do exercise in the loud music, carrying the player walking through streets in the sight of the eyes of people, at subway stations, on the streets, in front of any glass windows. Even at the extremely cold winter, he still wore that shabby rag, exposed his shiny bronze chest in the frozen wind, exercising, playing and walking.

Over the years, his personal style also developed, using a piece of rag to cover his body as usual, but he managed to add the tattoo of a skull on the chest, most importantly, he used a mask to cover his face which had an expression of mock smile, and some wild baby dolls hanging over the back. He always exposed his dark shiny body, there was only a small bag to cover his private part. When he was exercising, women would stop, laugh and scream. He became a mask man, infamous in this big city.

10. The Mask Man

On an extremely cold raining day in deep winter, in the heart of the city, few people were walking fast in the empty streets between the huge buildings, at one cross streets corner, loud music was overflowing on the air, broke the silent atmosphere, it was him, the mask man, standing in front of a glass wall, moving his heavy muscular body, watching himself through the reflection. The mock smile of the mask was teasing the passersby. This man showed a gesture of rejection to the world, he only wanted to be himself.

STORIES OF ROARS

This man showed a gesture of rejection to the world, he only wanted to be himself.

11. The Pigeons

No one knew her name, even herself almost forgot it.

She got up as usual, it was nine o'clock in the morning. Strong winter wind was howling all night, and diminished at daybreak. Before leaving, she put a hoodie over her head, dragged out a trolley. Last night she already filled it with pieces of bread. Her husband and son had left her to paradise in a tragedy years before, she was alone in this world, it was easy to die but hard to live without loved ones. As an old lady living alone, intentionally keeping distance with other people, to her, all of them were strangers, most of the time, she lived in her memory. When the weather was changing, because of the pain in her legs as well as arms, it would be difficult for her to walk. She managed to push the trolley out of the building, gasping for breath, looking around, this was her city in which she had been living for the most of her life here, knew every building, every corner of streets, she would notice even small changes here and there everyday. No one cared about her existence, she belonged to the past. Sometimes, she would remember her prime time in life, a smile would appear on her wrinkled face, it was her secret joy, those good memories gave her strength to go on in the present hard life.

Gentle breeze was playing with her hair, birds were chirping on the nearby trees. "It was a nice day!" She mumbled to herself, walking with a staggering gait. Although she was a lonely old lady, that day like everyday in those years, she was going to feed her children, the pigeons at different locations in the city, which was the purpose of her life for living, joy, happiness and consolation in the heart. It would be a good walk for hours, she did this day by day, if the weather permitted, she never stopped. She loved to see them. When they saw her, they would immediately fly to her, gaily walking around her with happy "gu gu gu..." sound, some even flying over her shoulders. She knew each one of them, the bold ones, the timid ones and the shy ones, She would make sure the weakest one also got its share.

On Broadway, a man was pissing at the street corner, then made a beast roar to the air: "Fuck! Fuck! Fuck!" Another man passed by, using a bar to smash everything in front of him, people were scared, and avoided him far away, and there was one more man who simply used his fists to punch people in front of him, a young man who did not avoid the sudden attack, was hit on the nose, who fell down on the pavement in intensive pain, using both his hands holding the face. Several Spanish women were selling Mexican food, one of them held a baby on her back, asking people to buy. A very old lady kept shouting: "God! God!..." She felt emotional pain, but helpless.

11. The Pigeons

The weather slowly changed, morning sunshine was replaced by gentle drizzle in the afternoon, she sat herself down on a roadside bench under a tree, gasping. She almost finished the task, only the last one left, which was located under a bridge by a highway. After this feeding, she would slowly go home.

The sky became clear again, she stood up, it costed her a lot of effort, the body pain made her feel hurt all the time. Pushing the trolley, she was approaching the bridge step by step, already seeing those hungry pigeons, she regarded them as her own children, waiting for her bread to feed. She did not realize that a man was following her silently, when he caught up, put her down on the ground, kicked her with both of his feet until she passed out. Before she totally lost her consciousness, saw her husband and son greeting her from the sky. The pain vanished, left the deadly quietness on the bloody spot.

STORIES OF ROARS

No one knew her name, even herself almost forgot it.

12. The Witch

I was walking in a misty wasteland.

Everything was as if in a dream, extremely silent, occasionally some beasts made roars in the nearby jungle. I did not worry about beasts, instead, I was very cautious about human's unpredictable behavior, just wanted to leave these strange surroundings, walking faster and faster.

I felt someone was following me, if I moved fast, it moved fast, if I moved slow, it moved slow. "What is the purpose of the follower?" I questioned myself. Suddenly it was getting closer to me, that was an old woman, an ugly one I had never seen in my life. Her eyes were sparkling with ghost light, deep as hell, with a prominent, sharp hook nose in the middle of the pale face. She was fully covered by a dark cloak, I could not perceive her body as well as her feet, she was floating in the wind, sometimes slow, sometimes fast. She quickly floated in front of me, saying: "Young man, where are you going?" Her voice was like the sound of splitting dry wood, then she chuckled viciously.

"Leave my way!" I shouted.

"What are you seeking?" She continued.

"I am seeking glory in the journey." I replied.

"Glory?" She mocked: "Do you think there is real glory in the world? It can only exist in the history books, truth is as ugly as my face. Those influential powerful people, their deeds were recorded by historians, but what were not recorded were those evil facts which were intentionally covered up. If you could open their brains to take a look at what they were really thinking, the dirtiness would be beyond your imagination. They used all means to satisfy their desires, from cheating to murder, and deceived the public so as to maintain a good name. Reputation is something most unreliable. Do you see that there is no real glory existing on earth any more, it is already tramped without a shape by the well known politicians as well as billionaires. We are in the dark era now. "

"I am also seeking wealth!" I disputed.

She laughed: "There are two kinds of wealth: The wealth of money and the wealth of spirit. About the first one, If you mean a decent life without poverty that is good, but if you talk about millions of dollars that must be connected with deceit, corruption and manipulation, an honest person can never be rich. Money is a very unfortunate matter in this world. Do you know how many good fellows because of money,

12. The Witch

turned inter evils, and how many people are suffering for the short of it? I have not seen a single billionaire without sins. Those who seek wealth lost their conscience, sold souls to Satan, going to marriage with power, setting rules to benefit themselves, in the meantime, forcing the majority into suffering from poverty. Do you see the rich commit a lot of immoral as well as cruel things, then donate a little portion of their money to gain a good name for covering their crimes. Why are there more and more roarers? They are the byproducts of the rich. Only if you are bad enough, you must understand that it is impossible to realize your goal; For the second one, people who seek for the wealth of spirit must have a noble soul, enduring countless difficulties and pain, including suffering from poverty, loneliness and misunderstanding, those are the most courageous human beings."

"I am also seeking beauty!" I argued.

She smiled when heard this: "Beauty is really a luscious matter, and the most valuable asset in life. Because it is useless, it is the most useful to humans. We can not continue to live if we lose the sense of beauty, a life without beauty is unbearable. People like poets, artists and musicians create beauty in human lives, they are the real backbones of mankind. It requires endless passion, imagination, devotion as well as love, those mean sacrifice. They build a firm bridge to the hopeful future for all mankind. Without them, all of us will remain in the darkness. Historians are not included in those people, there are very few truths inside their books, which always describe the favor of the powerful and wealthy. Scientists are a neutral group, the fruits of science only handled by humanists can have good results, otherwise will generate great disasters. The research and inventions they managed are poisoning, alienating and controlling people, take a look at the current pandemic and the destructive weapons. It is very possible one day in the future, humans will be eliminated by the science and technologies themselves created. There was a human saint of thinker called Schopenhauer proclaimed that human nature never could be improved, the bad would be always bad, which was absolutely true, considering Confucius tried hard to improve the nature of people thousands of years ago, today people are still not any better, if not any worse than their ancestors. We are divided by nations against each other, hating each other, creating national heroes, each one with its own justified reasons, but never know how to treat each other in a humane way. When we see movies, humans using all means, the most complicated tricks, intelligently, courageously, brutally fight against other human beings that are deeply rooted in our "civilized" culture. We are still ruled by the jungle rules: the strong eat the weak, just as the animals do at the wildness. What are we scared of? Other humans, what do we fight for? Still other humans. The waves of selfish desires will never stop, confined us as a brutal animal species. Look at those gold mine diggers, for gold, one can brutally kill the others as if to kill pigs. People honor the strong to be heroes instead of discard them for their cruel slaughter. We have two completely different stories about the current happenings from both sides to justify their own reasons. Hatred is occupying and the world is going to clash. Millions of people will die. Where do those roarers come from? They come from our society, from our daily suffering of life. Let me remind you, the extinction of mankind is inevitable, because mankind can not get rid of its sins, only the existence without sins can last forever. Humans are destined to

12. The Witch

be destroyed by their own scientific creation. When mankind is so proud of its wisdom, its stupidity is showing at the same time, science can do very little about it. As all humans have a maximum lifespan about one hundred thirty years, mankind also has an existence span, two hundred thousand years? Three hundred thousand years? Which we don't know yet, but the fate of mankind already hid when humans first came into beings to be finished on time. "

After the conversation, she added: "Young man, guard your way!" burst into long, dry laughter, there were green evil light shining in her eyes, a gust of wind blew her away, and disappeared in the fog.

Suddenly it was getting closer to me, that was an old woman, an ugly one I had never seen in my life.

13. The Station

Seven years before, Lucas made up a decision to leave Ecuador, his home town was close to the central ranges of the Andes bordering the Sierra, which constituted the country's highest and most continuous mountain chains. A lot of violent crime increased day by day because of poverty, especially after dark. Criminals targeted local taxis, buses, transport hubs and crowded areas. People kept vehicle doors and windows locked and valuables out of sight, even when moving, they were scared to go out, which made life very difficult. He wanted to leave chasing for hope and prosperity in the United States, passed the South Pacific Ocean by boat to Mexico with a group of people for the same hope, many of them were women and children. It was a dangerous travel, a lot of people were sick on the way, some even died, they finally reached Mexico. A Snakehead led them across the border entering the states from a river in the dark, his friend Miguel carried a baby, both of them drowned in the water in each other's arms. That painful memory occasionally would attack his mind. For all those years in New York, he had been working hard, saving money for the preparation to bring his wife and baby daughter here. He saw them on video calls, once in a week, normally Sundays, with the dream of living together as a joyful family. His heart was burning with hope.

Here was Queensboro Plaza, the key connection between Manhattan and Queens. Everyday thousands of trains were passing to and fro, thousands of people were passing by. That morning, he got up early to work, nothing special, it was a usual working day. At the station, one black man kept shouting: "marijuana, weed, please!" While walking around. Some South American Spanish immigrant women with little boys and little girls at the station begging people to buy cookies and chocolate, they were more and more recently. Every time he saw them, felt tortured and painful. A little girl about six years old was approaching him, holding a box of chocolate, her naive eyes looking up at his face. He perceived the misery of the world, but the little girl herself did not apprehend the meaning of misery at her age. He gave her one dollar, but did not take the chocolate, she reminded him of his own little girl. He never saw her in real life, she was born after he had left.

His floating mind drove him away from reality, the moments with his family warmed his thoughts, even that only on videos: "How lovely my little daughter is!" Something soft and wet moved his heart.

The train was approaching which dragged his attention back. What he did not realize was that there was a roarer, a bad one, who was standing behind him, watching him with cold blood,

13. The Station

pushing him from the back to the tracks. The driver tried to stop the train, but it was too late.

STORIES OF ROARS

What he did not realize was that there was a roarer, a bad one, who was standing behind him, watching him with cold blood, pushing him from the back to the tracks.

14. A Tortured Soul

I was standing outside of my home, and saw new sprouts had come out between the tree branches, which was a sign the hopeful beauty in the cycle of life has replaced the dead ugliness. The same rule could be placed in the human existence span.

So many tragic accidents have happened recently, unusual and bloody. There were three train crashes in one month: A train carrying fetal chemicals in Ohio went off the tracks affected thousands of animals, fish, and also local people in danger, more than one hundred thousand fish died shortly after that, animals like cows, deer, pigs etc. were sick and dying; a train and truck crash also in Ohio took place only few days later, followed by another crash occurred in Summers County, West Virginia yesterday. It was reported: "According to the county's 911 report, the train hit a boulder and fell into the local New River, catching fire after the violent collision."

STORIES OF ROARS

People looked around and asked: "What the hell is going on?"

It was a calm day. I was enjoying a cigar. Last night groups of raccoons were torn to death in the nearby neighborhoods, which invited some vultures hovering in the sky, some of them standing on the branches of trees, eager to share their meaty breakfast. Even jackals came from nowhere to the spots for meals. "The world is upside down, we all get fucked up!" Those thoughts were passing across my mind. If the world was not going to be better, it had to go worse.

A filthy man approached me: "Do you have a lighter?" he asked.

"No!" I replied. People were carrying diseases, besides I didn't want to contact strangers.

He was annoyed, saying: "How can you smoke a cigar without a lighter?"

I answered: "I don't owe you a lighter."

Then he asked: "Why do you look scared? What are you scared of?" meanwhile putting his hand over my chest to test the bumping of my heart, but found nothing.

He turned to a passerby for a lighter, lit a roll of weed, and seemingly enjoyed it. "Let me tell you some jokes." He said. "What the children looked like from a white and a black? And what the children looked like from a black and an Asian? And what the children looked like from an Asian and an Arabic?"

14. A Tortured Soul

I answered in a manner of refusal: "First of all, what you said is stupid and silly, secondly they are not jokes but questions, I don't like your questions." After that, I walked away.

In the following month I saw this man at different locations in the city, silently watching the flows of people in the transit. One day he came close to me again, trying to talk with me, but I stopped him: "I don't want to hear your stupid questions." I added: "I don't like you!"

He replied: "I like nobody!"

It was clear to me, a roarer was forming in his tortured soul.

STORIES OF ROARS

Then he asked: "Why do you look scared? What are you scared of?"

15. The Nights Were Moving

I met Greenman at a party in the upper part of Manhattan. People at the party were well beyond one hundred: artists, dancers, musicians, scientists and other walks of life. About one hour later, the atmosphere was soaring, two drunk men were naked, chasing each other in the hall. Guests were shocked at first, then amused, cheering and laughing. One of them was Greenman, who absolutely lost control at that moment, still kept asking for wine. Greenman was a man of strong thick build, with an expressive cockscomb head, wild beard. After the chaos, that night I went home with him because he was totally drunk. On the train he was laughing with himself, people were scared and kept away from him as far as possible. When I was leaving him, I asked: " Can you find the road going home by yourself?" He answered: "Don't worry." But that night he was on the subway all night, until woke up after daybreak.

He was a bass player in a rock team, they were playing at several different restaurants around the Greenwich area, but paid little, even difficult to survive, and kept doing only for the love of music. He stopped about two years later. I asked him why he discontinued his hobby, he said: " Not talented enough to make a future."

Later, I came across Greenman on a street in Queens. He greeted me far away: "Hi! what's up bro?" then holding my hand tightly, gave me a warm embrace. He invited me to his home for a drink. While walking, I looked at him secretly. He became much older than the last time I saw him, his beard grew even more wildly, some white hairs already appeared, considering he was only a little bit more than forty. The expression on his face showed a feeling of torment. His apartment was on the sixth floor. When we went inside and sat down, he asked: "What would you like: gin, brandy, vodka, grape wine or beer? I have all of them." I answered: "Ow, that was quite something!" Then we began to drink and talk.

"What were you doing all those years?" I asked.

"I was working on my freedom." He replied.

"Working on freedom? What does that mean?" I said.

He continued: "Do you realize all of us are manipulated by the system? The system keeps the majority alive and hungry, but never has enough money to live free. People are enslaved, unable to have a decent life, they are puppets of the rich who control the world, and don't realize where their sufferings come from, which come from the barbarian social system that benefits few while deploying the majority. We are far from

15. The Nights Were Moving

being civilized, humanity is still a future dream."

"But what does that have to do with your personal freedom?" I insisted.

"Let me explain to you." He said. "I can not save the world, at least I can find a way to save myself."

"How?"

"People used to listen to news, the basic principle of news is always one-sided story which they want you to listen to and believe that covers the fact of more important issues behind it, that is why one news from different people will have a different story. To capture the principles of the games of the ongoing world, one has to educate oneself from the very beginning, forget whatever people told you, and trust your own wisdom, working on it. You will find the truth hidden in society, and you will understand how they manipulate power to benefit their interest. Until you really comprehend the social rules, you can join the game to play for the sake of yourself."

"I still did not understand." I added.

"There are hiding rules behind the surface which you must search out, the points where you can thrust your own interest onto those places, and become a part of the functional game, once you manage that, you can not be fooled by the dominant players. Whenever a new technology comes into being, which could be your big chance to be one of the benefited people if you join early enough. The money people can make is the money they can think of."

He continued to say: "For example, in the case of crypto, I did full research on how it functions on the different resources, analyzed many cases in the market to grasp the secret rules before actually investing my money to play the game. I am working twenty four hours a day to closely study any changes of the tides up and down, investing twelve cryptocurrencies, buying and selling all the time to avoid traps on the market. In this barbarian world, only money can buy freedom, it is impossible to have freedom without money, I am working on it." When he was talking, there was a proud expression as well as self assurance in his tune.

I could easily see he was living a very simple life like a hermit, always sitting in front of his computer. We chatted for hours, no one noticed the darkness already engulfed the city, it was the time for me to leave.

I walked in the quiet streets under a starry deep blue sky, only passing by a few men. I carefully kept a distance from them, after all, I did not know who could be a dangerous roarer, especially at midnight. Most people were asleep, but wild cats were busy crossing streets here and there, it was the time for them hunting for food. "How many hungry tortured souls searching for freedom, struggling to survive in this devastated world!" I sighed to myself, still thinking the words Greenman talked with me. Greeman was seeking freedom, but what I saw was he had been tied up to the chair day in and day out, totally lost his freedom in his life.

15. The Nights Were Moving

Occasionally I went to parties with some friends, and became more solitary with the ages growing. It has been a long time since I met Greenman. At an evening party, one friend stood up, asked the others: "Have you guys heard something about our friend Greenman?" Seeing nobody replied, he continued: "I have some news about him, it was said that he got over one million dollars by trading on cryptocurrencies during the last two years. He was lucky!"

I knew how determined Greenman was at making money, if he became a millionaire, which was nothing to do with luck, but for his persistence made him rich. A man's will has won.

A few months later, I remembered it was a stormy night, wind was howling across streets, tree branches bumping on the window panes with scary sounds. I was sitting in my studio, in a dreaming condition, and did not care about the outside doomy world. With a glass of wine in my hand, I could feel heaven without worry despite the fact that we were miserable human beings. Suddenly there was a heavy knock on the door, then, another one. At that moment I was truly annoyed. Who would get out on such a terrible night? Reluctantly I got up from my chair, cursing the unexpected visitor. I put the lights on, unlocked the door. A heavy man stepped in, shaking first, then fell on the ground, who was no other than Greenman.

"My dear friend! What's up? Why do you appear like this?" I exclaimed.

"I come from hell." He answered with his voice rolling in the throat.

"Come on, bro, close to the fireplace, let us chat slowly." I tried to soothe him.

I accommodated him on a chair, holding him a glass of wine, and felt a little nervous: "Could you tell me what's going on?" I asked.

He buried his face in both hands, and sobbing: "I lost all the money in the market I had made, including my own money!" His voice was harsh and broken.

"How?"

"Over the past half year, the crypto market suddenly went down. I hoped it was temporary, but it wasn't, I had no choice but to wait, until it was down to hell. I did not fully realize the behind manipulation and schemes which I thought I had understood, moreover, I was too naive in believe the market analyses."

"You should have been more cautious my friend." I sighed.

"No! Bro, it was not because I did not act more cautiously, but because I was not bad enough to detect the darkness of those wicked hearts, only people bad enough could make big money, which was based on the suffering of others." Then he added: "Don't believe the news, don't believe the public, don't believe the social system, don't believe there is justice, don't believe anyone!"

His voice filled with indignation, I could see fire was burning in his soul. From then on, he was not only a hermit, but also a true

15. The Nights Were Moving

roarer who would dig the gold in the flame of hell. He would be burnt or become one of those wicked demons himself.

STORIES OF ROARS

I remembered it was a stormy night, wind was howling across streets, tree branches bumping on the window panes with scary sounds.

16. The Prophecy

The dividing line between reality and a dream is as thin as a transparent paper, reality could be a part of a dream, and a dream could be a part of reality, moreover, in some situations a dream is even more real than reality, and reality could be more like a dream.

It was a deep dark night, and also absolutely quiet, I could hear my own heart beating. However, I kept walking along a narrow alley hastily. A wild cat was running across the streets in front me, suddenly stopped, staring boldly at me. At the same time very cautious, knew that it could not trust a human being. In a moment it walked away, and disappeared behind a building. I did not know where I was going, and also the purpose of my action, but I did comprehend that I should never stop. Not long I saw myself at the dead end of the alley. On the top of a long pole, there was a bright light shining in the dark, illuminating everything nearby. Surprisingly I saw countless moths around the bright spot, all together flying to the bright center as waves.

STORIES OF ROARS

In fact they were going to the death, being burnt by the heat, falling down one after the other, occupied on the ground. Some of them died immediately, the others did not die struggling with torment, the ones regained strength would fly again to the hot bright light until absolutely burnt into death, helplessly flowing in the air, fell down to the tomb where thousands of dead moths already formed a hill on the ground. When I tried to look more closely, those moths have altered in the human shape in front of my eyes, full of desires, the desires for wealth, glory, ideal, even death could not stop them, even they were in extreme pain and suffering, everyone wanted to go first to the illuminated illusion of paradise.

"How ugly! How Stupid!" I was in dismay. Those was us, human beings, kidnapped by desires from cradle to the tomb, hopelessly hoped, even the obvious abyss in front of us, still jumped together, creating beautiful fantasy for each other, without thinking to switch the way for the future, never comprehended happiness could not be found in desires, never understood in the end, all of us would be empty handed, it was no meaning lost all happiness in struggling for temporary have.

16. The Prophecy

"*How ugly! How Stupid!*" *I was in dismay.*

17. Conversation With A Hermit

I already drove in the desert for more than five hours in total darkness, there was nothing outside the car, only occasionally saw a few solitary lights hanging on the isolated poles. The sound of running wheels touching the rough ground echoing in the air. I was on the way to pay a visit to a master thinker of our era who was living in the deep desert from nowhere. Finally I saw the sole hill whose silhouette against the dark sky, that was where he was living. driving on the circling earth trail around the hill, at the end of the road standing a tall steel gate of a huge mansion which had warm light radiating from several windows in front of me. I bumped the huge lock while shouting, waiting for someone to open the gate. It seemed a long time passed, I was quivering in the chilly wind of the night. In the dark, an Eskimo hound rushed out from a door of the mansion, barking at me inside the gate. An old lady appeared, scolding the dog to silence: "I Know you aren't used to seeing visitors, but this one is a guest of the master, don't make him scared!"

17. Conversation With A Hermit

I felt released to hear a human sound in this isolated land of the earth, it was scary. She opened the door, led me inside to the parlor. There was an old man sitting on a rocking chair beside the fireplace with a long white beard, I could not see his face. He did not stand up, but said to me: "Welcome my young friend from the outside world, you must have had a long tedious journey."

I sat myself down close to the old man with deep respect, who turned his face toward me, studying me with his eyes which were hidden in the dark shadow of the light. Not long after, the lady served me a cup of hot tea. I felt much more at home while drinking, carrying so many questions with me, hoping to get help from the wise thinker in front of me.

"I know you have got something in your mind, I am ready to hear and help." He said to me, as if I was his child.

Me: The fact that you are a unique thinker with a master mind at our times, I do have some questions and need answers, but no one can give any good advice to me except you. First, could you tell me why you retreat from the world?

The Hermit: I used to play with the tides of society. In those years I have seen so many tricks as well as ugliness in human activities, the world fell down step by step in front of my eyes. The good period of modern time was after The Second World War and before the pandemic, then the banquet was over, humans into brutal, chaotic conflicts all over the world. I realized that it was the time for me to retreat from this deeply troubled world because I did not have the power to do anything useful for mankind. I am just an eye witness and also an observer outside the current situation of the world, for the sake of understanding human nature and analyzing its fate. Science has done as much damage as help to humanity. I see the tendency of major superpowers to accumulate strength against each other, there will be a huge clash, a lot of blood will shed, death will fall at every corner of the earth. We all will sink to the darkest hell, the tragedy will be beyond our imagination.

Me: Do we have a chance to avoid the clash?

The Hermit: No! It belongs to a part of human fate because who we are and what we are doing. If something is inevitable, acceptance would be the only choice, please stay back and watch.

Me: When I was very young, I felt joyful and happy with hope, believing that with the development of science and technology, life would become better. For that reason, I studied hard, but now all that I have are wounds and pain in my heart, I don't believe in humanity anymore. This world is actually worse, contemporary life is not better at all than the past, people lost true emotions, acting like puppets, hatred is everywhere. There is no difference between the true and the fake any more from what we see and what we hear, everything can be made up by technologies, human beings have totally lost their privacy as well as identity. We are busy at work each day, have no time for enjoyment, but barely survive. Do you know the reason why this world is in such shitty corruption?

The Hermit: It is nurtured and rooted in the evil nature of

17. Conversation With A Hermit

mankind. When we are closer to death and in pain, we are also closer to the truth of life, but the time people are better off, they immediately forget all things that have learned from suffering, doing damage to each other again, this is the ugly fact about human nature. Brutality among the rich is a very common phenomenon, we saw poor people sharing the last bread, but never saw the rich sharing their extra money, if they do, it most likely another bigger game is going to play. Humans committed so many sins even God would feel shame about his creation. Maybe the evil has to grow with the growth of wisdom, like the darkness has to be at the side of the brightness, otherwise both of them can not exist. If this is true, to the end, humans will never be able to escape from suffering.

Me: Do you think mankind still has a future?

The Hermit: It is clear that there is no future for mankind fighting with each other, the only solution is to establish a social structure benefits for all, not for few so called corrupt elites, which can prevent the conflicts among people, that I can not see at the present condition and also in the near future, considering that the ugliness of human nature that deeply rooted in the genes. The beauty in mankind is so rare that is why we appreciate it so much. Do we have the ability to reform our brutal culture? I am very doubtful!

Moreover, the fortune in this world is already more than enough for all people to have a decent life. Why are there still so many people living in poverty? The rich always keep telling a big lie: if all people are living in good condition, they will lose the ability to be creative and become lazy. According to this theory, poverty is necessary! Suffering is necessary! Death is necessary! Creativity is deeply rooted in human personality, it has nothing to do with fortune. Creative people will always be creative in whatever life condition, lazy people will be lazy also in whatever life condition. I want to state clearly here: If there are too many poor people, that is evidence of failure in the social system.

I came here with hope, when I was leaving, hope already abandoned me.

17. Conversation With A Hermit

"I know you have got something in your mind, I am ready to hear and help." He said to me, as if I was his child.

18. The Kids

No one knew where he came from, and what his name was, even himself did not know, because he had totally lost his mind. He always stayed outside of a McDonald. The way he looked was very rough, dirty and wild. However, he carried a flute with him, from time to time playing solitary romantic melodies, showing that he magically kept a tender part in his soul, memorizing his lost love, or cherishing some warm family moments in the past? Even in this winter time, gusty wind blew over trash turning on the streets, when people heard his play, would stop, partially fascinated, partially wondered.

That day when he was playing, three kids were passing by. They were little roarers, watched at him for a while, amused. The first kid came up, padded him on the head, and ran away. The second kid kicked him on the leg, also ran away. The third kid took the flute from his hands, trying to escape. This time he was prepared himself, he grasped the boy, kept punching the

18. The Kids

boy on the face until he fell down. People were screaming, no one dared to come up.

When the cops came to the spot, the little boy had passed away.

No one knew where he came from, and what his name was, even himself did not know, because he had totally lost his mind.

19. The Wanderer

New York is a strange city, only has two seasons: summer and winter. The switch between summer and winter is only a few days away, there is no spring and autumn, and the temperature in one day also changes dramatically. Like the weather, people living here are also unpredictable.

It was a beautiful evening, the glow of sunset reflected in the backyard, rustling leaves were waving in the gentle breeze. I was in a good mood, temporarily forgetting the suffering of life. A cup of tea was ready on the table. That night I wanted to be free in the little slice of life, enjoy reading. What I wanted to read was The Murders in the Rue Morgue, a story by Edgar Allan Poe, who deeply revealed the decay of human nature a long time ago, the evil intention of human desires. I occasionally sharpened my thoughts through reading. There were urgent knocks on my door, Felt annoyed because I did not want to accommodate visitors at that cozy moment. Who was there?

STORIES OF ROARS

It was Jeffery, a long time friend of mine. He came inside, immediately sat himself down deeply in the rocking chair. He was a happy person, very talkative, but that moment I saw sorrow and silence on his face. I did not ask him, waiting for him to tell me.

"I came back home last night from North Carolina. When I opened the door, Daysie refused to let me enter, she said I often left and came back without noticing her, and treated the home as a hotel." Daysie was his wife, she was very mad with him for his unpredictable behavior.

After the short words, He fell in silence again. After five minutes he said: " It's gone."

That was Jeffery, always taking everything easy, nothing in the world could put him down. Could you imagine, he only needed five minutes to get rid of serious family issues? We have been friends for a long time, he never could stay in one place, always traveling, and often changing his mind in one second. Years before he spent five hundred dollars to buy a shabby car, living in the car, traced from city to city all over America. I liked to hear his unusual roadside stories. He was very open minded, an attentive listener, with curiosity about any new things. Because of that, he met a lot of people, made many friends from all walks of life: Mormons, actresses, professors, whores, writers, artists, drug addicts and so on. He lived his life of a modern bohemian style. That night we both lay down comfortably on chairs, straight for hours in the dim light, chatting with warm romantic imagination. We talked about art, literature, and the old days of the past. Meanwhile he took out a thick notebook

19. The Wanderer

from his pocket to show me, which had detailed records in small words page by page about all the interesting things that happened when he was traveling. He told me he would use the information to write a traveler's novel one day in the future. I encouraged him to do so, saying that which could be the most interesting, as well as romantic book in the world.

Time eclipsed quickly, it was already after midnight. Jeffery suddenly stood up: "I will go to Maryland."

I asked: "How? In such a deep night?"

He replied: "You don't know, The airplane companies have Red Time flights which are very cheap, the time most people will not go. The only inconvenience is that they are indirect flights, always going round about, for example, in the case I go to Maryland, they will carry me to Chicago or somewhere else first, that will cost much more time which I don't care about, I will sleep on the plane."

"Even so, how can you find a place to stay at night?" I still thought his decision was crazy.

"Every city has free shelters I know very well, and I have some special friends who can provide a lodge for me to stay." He seemed pretty sure about everything.

I had nothing to say anymore, knew that if he made a decision, no one could change his mind. He opened the door, disappeared in the dark.

STORIES OF ROARS

Before night I lived in a daydream condition each day, but after the darkness, I was very active with my brain: painting, writing, reading. Sometimes I would walk alone in the dark street by street for hours. Of course I was very careful avoiding those dangerous roarers.

One month later, Jeffery came back, this time he looked different, his eyes were shining with joy: "I found love, real love!" He proclaimed.

I knew he met a lot of women, and had intimate relationships with most of them, but I never believed in his world, there was a place for love.

"What has happened?" I asked.

"That night, when I arrived in Maryland, the sky was still dark. I went and knocked on an old lady's house, we were long time friends. She was very happy to accommodate me, we had an intimate affection for each other, sometimes we would take bath together, I felt at home side by side with her aged body. She loved to touch and kiss me tenderly, but we were not lovers, she regarded me as her son, just felt good with each other's companions. Several days later I left her for another city in North Virginia. One day I was idly strolling on the street, and saw a pleasant girl sitting on the stairs in front of a house. After greeting her, I went up and had a casual chat with her. When I was about to leave, I gave her my phone number and said: "If you want to, call me to have a cup of coffee together." She really called the next day, we were so passionate with each other. It was the first time I felt real love!"

19. The Wanderer

"How about your wife?" I said.

"The marriage died a long time ago, she will be very glad to get rid of me."

As he said, they got divorced in one month without any trouble. The next time I saw him, Jeffery showed me his ring on his finger in a very happy mood from the new marriage, looking like a real happy man. I continued to visit his new family occasionally, there was a lot of harmony between them. Not long after, a girl was born, then a boy also came into the family. It was a great pleasure for me to see them with the children. I began to believe they had real love. His new wife named Neva, who told me secretly: "I searched for more than twenty years to find my true love!" In this world, nothing could be happier than seeing two persons in real love!

One evening, I went with a friend to visit Jeffery Family to congratulate them on just moving into a new apartment, but they were not happy at all, because Jeffery hurt his spine when moving the furniture. He was helplessly lying down in the bed, the wife was sobbing as if in deep suffering. There was not too much to say, and nothing could be done to help. We left early. Fortunately he recovered after one month. Neva has taken good care of him.

In the next few years, I saw Jeffery and his wife together at parties, museums, gallery openings, strolling at Central Park, sometimes with their children, sometimes by themselves. It was obviously a happy family, but I didn't anticipate that nothing could change the nature of a human's desires.

I was very surprised when Jeffery told me privately one time: "I feel bored in the present life, I am going to look for another woman, she must be a very different type from my wife Neva.

He was a kind person, but could not afford a normal life. Betrayal was a part of his passion.

19. The Wanderer

He was a kind person, but could not afford a normal life. Betrayal was a part of his passion.

20. The Day

On the side of a highway , there was a cemetery that was as big as a few miles wide. On the side of the cemetery, there was a bus stop where he went to wait for the shuttle bus to the city. Since he came here, things have changed a lot, not better, but much worse. So many roarers were out there, no one felt safe in daily life any more. Every time he went out, would be very cautious about the surroundings.

His home was nearby, it could be reached in five minutes on foot from the bus stop. On a usual day, he liked to walk silently, to feel the fences on the roadside, flowers, wild weeds and fallen leaves, as if a kind of ritual in the course of life. Sometimes in the harsh winter, the violent wind blew over, as to tear off the chest of the earth, when the cold wind hit his face like needles, he felt a painful relief, because this pain awakened the vitality in the instinct of his nature, the numbness in life was the matter he hated most. Going to the station when the sun was shining, he would try his best to put a joyful feeling in his heart, recalling

20. The Day

the beautiful moments in his earlier life, reliving all the way in his heart.

Sometimes it took a long time for the bus to come, so he began to study the cemetery. If it was on a clear day, the cemetery was floating in a lazy, comfortable atmosphere, making people feel that death was not a terrible matter at all, but an enviable beauty; when on a day of raining and windy to come here, the chilly feeling in the bones made him want to escape from this gloomy place as soon as possible, without staying even a moment. Even though from the lessons of his life, he understood the real devils were not the dead, but the people carrying a heart with hatred.

There were many flowers in the cemetery, also huge aged trees. The watcher's house of the tombs was a two-story building, which was located in the shades of several huge trees. At dusk, the warm red lights in the several windows turned it into a fascinating home. The endless tombstones varied in sizes and shapes. Some of the tombstones were decorated with flowers, the others were placed with flower baskets or garlands. The inscriptions on the tombstones were similar: name, date of birth and death, parents, brothers and sisters etc, text as: "May you get a good home in heaven!" "We will always love you!" "Dear, you are our forever missing." There was also someone special: "Please wait patiently, we will meet again in the Kingdom of Heaven!" Usually when people were getting older, they were not scared about death, but regarded it as a chance to escape from this terrible world, a chance to have a permanent peace and be reborn.

Bus came, today there was a black driver, he got on the bus

with difficulty. Because it was sunny, the driver was in a good mood, forgot driving rules, and chatted with a passenger near him. The bus was moving on a winding road, houses on both sides continued to cross bus windows to the rear. Recently, he had been unable to distinguish the difference between dream and reality, always feeling that he was in a dream. Life had an unreal, vain, absurd feeling. When he dreamed at night, it felt very real. Before a highway bridge, suddenly there were people running outside, they were very scared, shouting and screaming. The sound of gunshots echoing in the air, several shots penetrated the bus window panes, people in the bus were scared, helplessly cursing the world. The driver increased speed to leave the scene, lucky, no one got hurt.

Subway was very crowded. After a while, a few Mexicans wearing wide-brimmed straw hats stood in the passage and played music. Although he couldn't understand Spanish, he knew that it was a love song, one of them held a straw hat and began to seek donations one by one. They just left, came in a pregnant woman, looked sad, complaining that she was sick, had no money for hospital, had an unemployed husband, and several children needed to be fed. This situation had been staged almost every day in the subway, and people became used to it. Buddha had said life was suffering, it was confirmed here.

That day, he wanted to stay in the city for a few hours, went in and out of the city, repeatedly left and returned, like the cycle of life and death. In this way, life was cut into many fragments and was constantly replayed.

He was very familiar with every square of the streets here,

20. The Day

which had little change in the decades he had been here. It was very busy on a normal day, but today it was surprisingly quiet, pedestrians were few. The city seemed to have taken its heart out.

Every day, a limp old woman pushed a trolley and turned herself here. The plastic bags in the trolley were filled with bread. She smashed the bread and sprinkled it on the ground. Flocks of pigeons flew down for food. She gasped a few breaths, then went to other places to finish the same task, going back and forth for decades. Her persistent behavior evoked his curiosity: Did she have a family? Why did she do this accurately every day? Once he had tried to talk to her, didn't anticipate the old lady looking at him with vigilance, as if an intruder suddenly broke into her territory, left with self muttering, he never bothered her again after that.

From time to time, the tragedies and comedies of the world were staged here. Shooting incidents occurred many times beside him; a magician did amazing performances; an old woman dressed as a cowgirl, holding a guitar, a pair of loose breasts fell down on her chest, already lost water, whose aged skin was like bark of a tree, only had a sling between her legs, had lost the feeling of shame. Next to her, there were naked young women with huge breasts, as well as fat hips, fresh in prime, had long, red or blue feathers on their heads, and only used a piece of cloth to cover the important private parts, proudly standing there, attracting tourists to take photos. He remembered that many years ago, an extremely cold winter night, more than ten degrees beneath zero, came here a group of nudists, lingering in the square as if nothing, who had claimed on the radio news to challenge the limits of physical body, attracted a lot of onlookers.

In this richest part of the world, there were homeless people everywhere. Beggars in his native country would act very tragically, but the beggars here never forgot the power of humor. One of the cardboards placed on the street side, wrote: "Why lie? just want money to have a beer." The other one wrote: "Money, drugs, sex, power, we corrupt together." Even more drama one: "My family has been killed by aliens, that is why I am here." A few policemen came over and said angrily: "Put it up, just ask for money, why mess it up with a big lie?"

The sky became doom again, it was time to go back home. He walked to the direction of the subway entrance, trying to find his way between cartoon figures, they were everywhere in the city, eager to grasp people nearby to take photos with them. There was a group of homelessness sitting down at a street corner. One of them stood up, looking at the pedestrians, his eyes sparkling with fire, making a big roar, pounding his chest with hands: "I am strong! I am strong!" He shouted repeatedly. The others were chanting:

We are the kingdom of the homeless,

Let the sun fall into pieces,
   Let wind blow in blood,
   Let fire burn without mercy,
   Let heart cry without emotions,
   Let the world be broken without rescue.

20. The Day

Come and go, come and go,
   This world is as beautiful as hell.

Falling! Falling! Falling!

After the chant, all of them burst into laughter. He did not pay too much attention to them, as far as he knew, most of them had gone out of mind. He was happy the subway entrance was already in front of his eyes, ready to go down.

Suddenly a lot of people were running out in panic. One guy jumped out, pushing a man in front of him, when the man was falling down, who pushed down another, in a moment, many people were falling down on the ground, and kept struggling. An old lady was weeping, her bag was thrown away, the stuff in the bag spread all over the entrance, no one noticed her, not to mention to help. He heard intense gun fires inside the station. Several cops holding guns rushed down the entrance. Another burst of gunshots, then the place became deadly silent, even the cries of people were soundless. Everyone tried to have self control at this terrible moment. It was told the shooting men inside the station exchanged fire with policemen, and were killed on the spot.

Three hours later he was permitted to board the train going home. "What a tragic day!" He thought by himself, still felt the tension in his mind. Being safe he had a mood of fortunate. The train was running past several stations, in one hour he should be home again without worry, but it was still running in the tunnel.

No one had expected the train to suddenly stop. For a long time it did not move, people were out of patience, cursing with dirty words. The conductor finally made an announcement, there was a man standing between the tracks, he was waiting for the policemen to come here to help. Cursing, coughing, babies' crying, when the policemen came to the train, they needed time to reach the person and move him from the tracks. The conductor made an announcement again, saying in order to move the person from the tracks, electricity had to take off.

And then, people were staying in darkness, waiting and waiting.

20. The Day

Let the sun fall into pieces,
Let wind blow in blood,
Let fire burn without mercy,
Let heart cry without emotions,
Let the world be broken without rescue.

21. The Bell

I heard the bell of the church, but I did not believe the soothing sound could end the grief of the world.

We live, we suffer, we die.

21. The Bell

We live, we suffer, we die.

Epilogue

Those years in New York City, I encountered so many roarers, some had pure souls, kind, harmless, and unique within themselves; others had dirty minds, extremely aggressive and dangerous. Yes! I was helpless being forced to observe those scenes of ugliness and bloodiness. People were helpless, society was helpless, the world was helpless.

In the AI era, the trust among mankind is destined to lose. When humans totally distrust each other, the end of mankind is nearby. At this moment, I still can not see the possibility of any positive changes happening. As human beings, we are falling down together, to hell.

This book is just a reminder of the cataclysmic death-dealing process to mankind.

Epilogue

This book is just a reminder of the cataclysmic death-dealing process to mankind.

About the Author

Shutao Liao, born on 25th August 1963, Zigong, Sichuan, China. He received Raffaello Sanzio Master Award, Shakespeare Award and Nelson Mandela Human Value Award in 2014, Honorary Master Member of Italian Cultural Association 2014, Honorary Master Member of Academy of Visual Art "Italia In Arte Nel Mondo" Cultural Association 2016. He is a world acclaimed artist, writer, poet and humanist.

His recent study was focused on the decay of humanity.

You can connect with me on:
🌐 https://liaoshutao.blogspot.com

Milton Keynes UK
Ingram Content Group UK Ltd.
UKHW041654151024
449742UK00005B/35